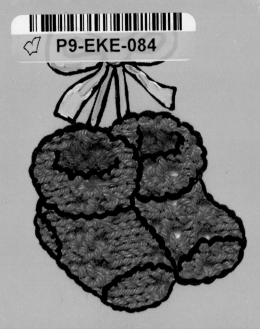

What does Ian eat?
What does the baby eat?

What does Ian wear on his feet?
Which clothes belong to the baby?

What does Ian play with?
And what does the baby play with?

Which cup belongs to Mom?
And which cup belongs to Ian?

Where does the baby sleep?

First published in Belgium and Holland by Clavis Uitgeverij, Hasselt – Amsterdam, 2015
Copyright © 2015, Clavis Uitgeverij

English translation from the Dutch by Clavis Publishing Inc. New York
Copyright © 2016 for the English language edition: Clavis Publishing Inc. New York

Visit us on the web at www.clavisbooks.com

Big Brother Ian written and illustrated by Pauline Oud
Original title: *Kas wordt grote broer*
Translated from the Dutch by Clavis Publishing

ISBN 978-1-60537-258-7

This book was printed in December 2015 at Publikum d.o.o., Slavka Rodica 6, Belgrade, Serbia

First Edition
10 9 8 7 6 5 4 3 2 1

Big Brother **Ian**

Pauline Oud

Clavis
NEW YORK

"Look how big Mommy's belly is!
It looks like a balloon!" says Ian.
"Hello, who is in that belly?
Baby, are you ready yet?"

Sometimes Flap sits on Mommy's belly.
Then her belly looks like a chair.
"That big belly is all mine," says Ian.
And he puts his ear against Mommy's belly.

"Look at that big cup," says Ian.
"It's mine.
But who is that little bottle for?
Who will drink from that?"

"Oh," says Ian, "I know!
That little bottle is for me. I can play with it.
Flap is still very small, and he likes to drink
from such a little bottle!"

"Look at that big sweater," says Ian. "It's mine. But who is that little top for? Who will wear that?"

"Oh," says Ian, "I know!
That little top is for me.
I can play with it.
Flap is still very small, and he can wear the little top."

"Look at that big bed," says Ian.
"It's mine.
But who is that little cradle for?
Who will sleep in there?"

"Oh," says Ian, "I know! That little cradle is for me. I can play with it. Flap is still very small, and he likes to sleep in the little cradle."

"Look at that big tub," says Ian.
"It's mine.
But who is that little tub for?
Who will bathe in that?"

"Oh," says Ian, "I know!
That little tub is for me.
I can play with it.
Flap is still very small, and he
likes to bathe in the little tub."

"Look at that big chair," says Ian.
"It's mine.
But who is that little seat for?
Who will sit on that?"

"Oh," says Ian, "I know!
That little seat is for me.
I can play with it.
Flap is still very small, and he
likes to sit on the little seat."

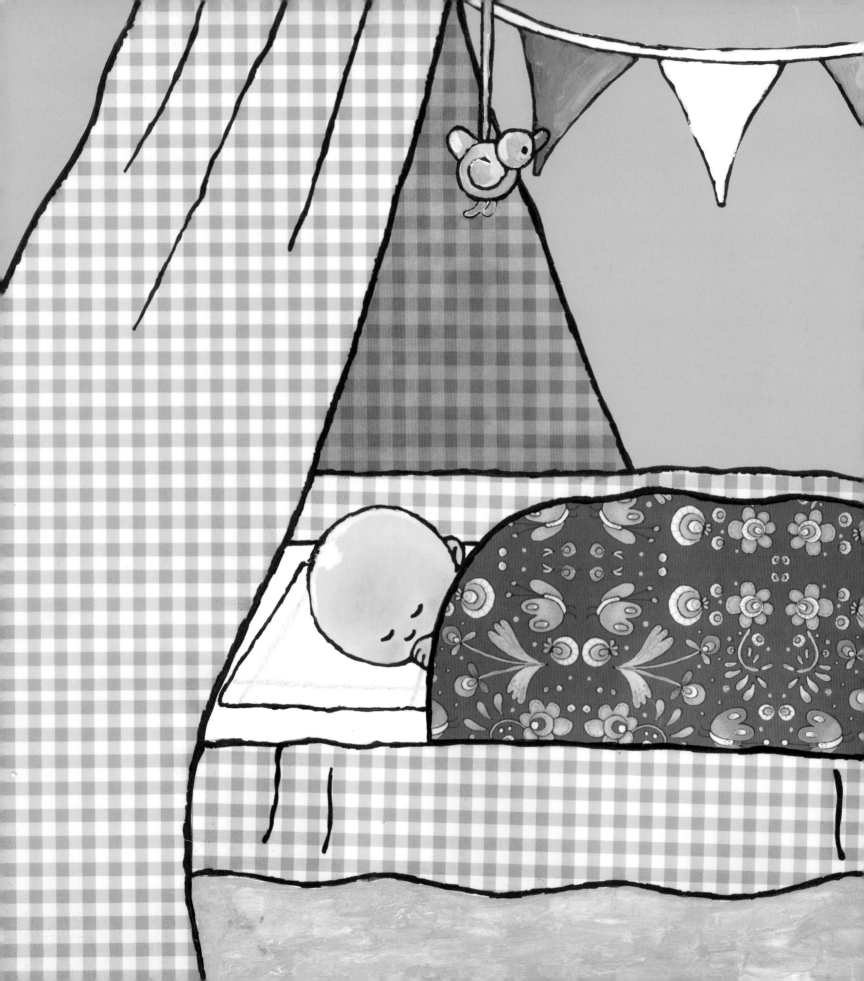

"Look," says Mommy,
"this is the baby.
Gently, don't wake it up."
Yes, Ian knows!
The baby came out of Mommy's belly.
Now Mommy's big belly has gone.
The baby is still very small and likes
to sleep in the little cradle.

"Look," says Mommy, "the baby is bathing."
Its little tush and tummy are getting all wet.
The baby is still very small and likes the
little bath. After the bath we put on the little
top and give the baby milk from the little bottle.
Then the baby goes back into the little cradle
and sleeps for a very long time."

The baby is lying on Mommy's lap.
Ian is not happy. *Mommy is mine*, he thinks.
Her lap was the perfect size for Flap and me.
"Baby, move up, I want to lie there too!"

Ian angrily kicks his toys away.
"Darn!" he says. "Now I know.
Everything belongs to the baby.
I can't play with anything anymore!"

But what happens?
It makes the baby happy!
The baby laughs, and laughs again.
And Ian isn't angry anymore.

Ian can make the baby laugh.
He knows how.
"Oh," says Ian. "I know!
I'll get my ball."

"Look at that big ball," says Ian.
"That ball is mine."
Then he shows the baby how to roll the ball.
The baby is still very small,
but Ian loves being a big brother!

Ian, Flap, and the baby are sitting on Mommy's lap.
It feels nice and cozy.
"Oh!" Ian says. "I know!
The little bottle and cradle belong to the baby.
And the little top, the little bath, and the little seat too.
But the baby," he says happily, "is all mine."